MR. MEN

MR. MEN

MR. MEN

MR. MEN

This book
belongs to:
. . . .

Original creation by Roger Hargreaves
Illustrated by Adam Hargreaves
First published in Great Britain 2003
This edition reissued in 2007 by Egmont UK Limited
239 Kensington High Street, London W8 6SA
ISBN 978 0 6035 6304 1
1 3 5 7 9 10 8 6 4 2
Printed in China

www.mrmen.com

MR. MEN
Story Treasury

by Roger Hargreaves

Contents

MR. TICKLE

by Roger Hargreaves

MR. TICKLE

It was a warm, sunny morning.

In his small house at the other side of the wood Mr Tickle was asleep.

You didn't know that there was such a thing as a Tickle, did you?

Well, there is!

Tickles are small and round and they have arms that stretch and stretch and stretch.

Extraordinary long arms!

Mr Tickle was fast asleep. He was having a dream. It must have been a very funny dream because it made him laugh out loud, and that woke him up.

He sat up in bed, stretched his extraordinary long arms, and yawned an enormous yawn.

Mr Tickle felt hungry, so do you know what he did?

He reached out one of his extraordinary long arms, opened the bedroom door, reached down the stairs, opened the kitchen door, reached into the kitchen cupboard, opened the biscuit tin, took out a biscuit, brought it back upstairs, in through the bedroom door and back to Mr Tickle in bed.

As you can see, it's very useful indeed having arms as long as Mr Tickle's.

Mr Tickle munched his biscuit. He looked out of the window.

"Today looks very much like a tickling day," he thought to himself.

So, later that morning, after Mr Tickle had made his bed and cooked his breakfast, he set off through the wood.

As he walked along, he kept his eyes very wide open, looking for somebody to tickle.

Looking for anybody to tickle!

Eventually Mr Tickle came to a school.

There was nobody about, so, reaching up his extraordinary long arms to a high window ledge, Mr Tickle pulled himself up and peeped in through the open window.

Inside he could see a classroom.

There were children sitting at their desks, and a teacher writing on the blackboard.

Mr Tickle waited a minute and then reached in through the window.

Mr Tickle's extraordinary long arm went right up to the teacher, paused, and then - tickled!

The teacher jumped in the air and turned round very quickly to see who was there.

But there was nobody there!

Mr Tickle grinned a mischievous grin.

He waited another minute, and then tickled the teacher again.

This time he kept on tickling until soon the teacher was laughing out loud and saying, "Stop it! Stop it!" over and over again.

All the children were laughing too at such a funny sight.

There was a terrible pandemonium.

Eventually, Mr Tickle thought that he had had enough fun, so he gave the teacher one more tickle for luck, and then very quietly brought his arm back through the open window.

Chuckling to himself, he jumped down from the window, leaving the poor teacher to explain what it was all about.

Which of course he couldn't.

Then Mr Tickle went to town.

And what a day Mr Tickle had.

He tickled the policeman on traffic duty at the crossroads in the middle of town.

It caused an enormous traffic jam.

He tickled the greengrocer just as he was piling apples neatly in his shop window.

The greengrocer fell over backwards, and the apples rolled all over the shop.

At the railway station, the guard was about to wave his flag for the train to leave.

As he lifted his arm in the air, Mr Tickle tickled him.

And every time he tried to wave his flag, Mr Tickle tickled him until the train was ten minutes late leaving the station and all the passengers were furious.

That day Mr Tickle tickled everybody.

He tickled the doctor.

He tickled the butcher.

He even tickled old Mr Stamp, the postman, who dropped all his letters into a puddle.

Then Mr Tickle went home.

Sitting in his armchair in his small house at the other side of the wood, he laughed and laughed every time he thought about all the people he had tickled.

So, if you are in any way ticklish, beware of Mr Tickle and those extraordinary long arms of his.

Just think. Perhaps he's somewhere about at this very moment while you're reading this book.

Perhaps that extraordinary long arm of his is already creeping up to the door of this room.

Perhaps it's opening the door now and coming into the room.

Perhaps, before you know what is happening, you will be well and truly . . .

. . . tickled!

MR. HAPPY

by Roger Hargreaves

On the other side of the world, where the sun shines hotter than here, and where the trees are a hundred feet tall, there is a country called Happyland.

As you might very well expect everybody who lives in Happyland is as happy as the day is long. Wherever you go you see smiling faces all round. It's such a happy place that even the flowers seem to smile in Happyland.

And, as well as all the people being happy, all the animals in Happyland are happy as well.

If you've never seen a mouse smile, or a cat, or a dog, or even a worm - go to Happyland!

This is a story about someone who lived there who happened to be called Mr Happy.

Mr Happy was fat and round, and happy!

MR. HAPPY

He lived in a small cottage beside a lake at the foot of a mountain and close to a wood in Happyland.

One day, while Mr Happy was out walking through the tall trees in those woods near his home, he came across something which was really rather extraordinary.

There in the trunk of one of the very tall trees was a door.

Not a very large door, but nevertheless a door. Certainly a door. A small, narrow yellow door.

Definitely a door!

"I wonder who lives here?" thought Mr Happy to himself, and he turned the handle of that small, narrow, yellow door.

The door wasn't locked and it swung open quite easily.

Just inside the small, narrow, yellow door was a small, narrow, winding staircase, leading downwards.

Mr Happy squeezed his rather large body through the rather thin doorway and began to walk down the stairs.

The stairs went round and round and down and down and round and down and down and round.

Eventually, after a long time, Mr Happy reached the bottom of the staircase.

He looked around and saw, there in front of him, another small, narrow door. But this one was red.

Mr Happy knocked at the door.

"Who's there?" said a voice. A sad, squeaky sort of voice. "Who's there?"

Mr Happy pushed open the red door slowly, and there, sitting on a stool, was somebody who looked exactly like Mr Happy, except that he didn't look happy at all.

In fact he looked downright miserable.

"Hello," said Mr Happy. "I'm Mr Happy."

"Oh, are you indeed," sniffed the person who looked like Mr Happy but wasn't. "Well, my name is Mr Miserable, and I'm the most miserable person in the world."

"Why are you so miserable?" asked Mr Happy.

"Because I am," replied Mr Miserable.

"How would you like to be happy like me?" asked Mr Happy.

"I'd give anything to be happy," said Mr Miserable. "But I'm so miserable I don't think I could ever be happy," he added miserably.

Mr Happy made up his mind quickly. "Follow me," he said.

"Where to?" asked Mr Miserable.

"Don't argue," said Mr Happy, and he went out through the small, narrow, red door.

Mr Miserable hesitated, and then followed.

Up and up the winding staircase they went. Up and up and round and round and up and round and round and up until they came out into the wood.

"Follow me," said Mr Happy again, and they both set off through the wood back to Mr Happy's cottage.

Mr Miserable stayed in Mr Happy's cottage for quite some time. And during that time the most remarkable thing happened.

Because he was living in Happyland Mr Miserable ever so slowly stopped being miserable and started to be happy.

His mouth stopped turning down at the corners.

And ever so slowly it started turning up at the corners.

And eventually Mr Miserable did something that he'd never done in the whole of his life.

He smiled!

And then he chuckled, which turned into a giggle, which became a laugh. A big booming hearty huge giant large enormous laugh.

And Mr Happy was so surprised that he started to laugh as well. And both of them laughed and laughed.

They laughed until their sides hurt and their eyes watered.

Mr Miserable and Mr Happy laughed and laughed and laughed and laughed.

They went outside and still they laughed.

And because they were laughing so much everybody who saw them started laughing as well. Even the birds in the trees started to laugh at the thought of somebody called Mr Miserable who just couldn't stop laughing.

And that's really the end of the story except to say that if you ever feel as miserable as Mr Miserable used to you know exactly what to do, don't you?

Just turn your mouth up at the corners.

Go on!

MR. STRONG

by Roger Hargreaves

MR. STRONG

This is the story of Mr Strong.

Mr Strong is the strongest person in the whole wide world.

The strongest person there has ever been, and probably the strongest person there ever will be.

He is so strong he can not only bend an iron bar with his bare hand, he can tie knots in it.

Mr Strong is so strong he can throw a cannonball as far as you or I can throw a tennis ball!

MR. STRONG

Mr Strong is so strong he can hammer nails into a wall by tapping them with his finger.

Strong by name and strong by nature!

And would you like to know the secret of Mr Strong's strength?

Eggs!

The more eggs Mr Strong eats, the stronger he becomes.

Stronger and stronger and stronger!

MR. STRONG

Anyway, this story is about a funny thing that happened to Mr Strong one day.

That morning he was having breakfast.

And for Breakfast he was having . . . eggs!

Followed by eggs. And to finish, he was having - guess what?

That's right. Eggs!

That was Mr Strong's normal breakfast.

After his eggy breakfast Mr Strong cleaned his teeth.

And, as usual, he squeezed all the toothpaste out of the tube.

And, as usual, he cleaned his teeth so hard he broke his toothbrush.

Mr Strong gets through a lot of toothpaste and toothbrushes!

MR. STRONG

After that he decided to take a walk.

He put on his hat and opened the front door of his house. Crash!

"What a beautiful day," he thought to himself and, stepping outside his house, he shut his front door.

Bang! The door fell off its hinges.

Mr Strong gets through a lot of front doors!

Then Mr Strong went for his walk.

He walked through the woods.

But, he wasn't looking where he was going, and walked slap bang into a huge tree. Crack!

The huge tree snapped and the tree thundered to the ground.

"Whoops!" said Mr Strong.

MR. STRONG

He walked into town.

And again, not looking where he was going, he walked slap bang straight into a bus.

Now, as you know, if you or I were to walk into a bus, we'd get run over.

Wouldn't we?

Not Mr Strong!

The bus stopped as if it had run into a brick wall.

"Whoops!" said Mr Strong.

Eventually Mr Strong walked through the town and out into the country. To a farm.

The farmer met him in the road looking very worried.

"What's the matter?" asked Mr Strong.

"It's my cornfield," replied the farmer. "It's on fire and I can't put it out!"

Mr Strong looked over the hedge, and sure enough the cornfield was blazing fiercely.

"Water," said Mr Strong. "We must get water to put out the fire!"

"But I don't have enough water to put a whole field out," cried the worried farmer, "and the nearest water is down at the river, and I don't have a pump!"

"Then we'll have to find something to carry the water," replied Mr Strong.

"Is that your barn?" he asked the farmer, pointing to a barn in another field.

"Yes, I was going to put corn in it," said the farmer. "But . . ."

"Can I use it?" asked Mr Strong.

"Yes, but . . ." replied the perplexed farmer.

Mr Strong walked over to the barn, and then do you know what he did?

He picked it up. He actually picked up the barn!

The farmer couldn't believe his eyes.

MR. STRONG

Then Mr Strong carried the barn, above his head, down to the river.

Then he turned the barn upside down.

Then he lowered it into the river so that it filled up with water.

Then, and this shows how strong Mr Strong is, he picked it up and carried it back to the blazing cornfield.

Mr Strong emptied the upside down barn full of water over the flames.

Sizzle. Sizzle. Splutter. Splutter.

One minute the flames were leaping into the air. The next minute they'd gone.

MR. STRONG

"However can I thank you?" the farmer asked Mr Strong.

"Oh, it was nothing," remarked Mr Strong modestly.

"But I must find some way to reward you," said the farmer.

"Well," said Mr Strong, "you're a farmer, so you must keep chickens."

"Yes, lots," said the farmer.

"And chickens lay eggs," went on Mr Strong, "and I rather like eggs!"

"Then you shall have as many eggs as you can carry," said the farmer, and took Mr Strong to the farmyard.

Mr Strong said goodbye to the farmer, and thanked him for his eggs, and the farmer thanked him for helping.

Then Mr Strong, just using one finger, picked up the eggs and went home.

MR. STRONG

Mr Strong put the eggs carefully down on his kitchen table and went to close the kitchen door.

Crash! The door fell off its hinges.

"Whoops!" said Mr Strong, and sat down.

Crunch! The chair fell to bits.

"Whoops!" said Mr Strong, and started cooking his lunch. And for lunch he was starting with eggs. Followed by an egg or two. And then eggs. And then for his pudding he was having . . .

Well, can you guess?

. . . Ice cream!
Ha! Ha!

MR. SILLY

by Roger Hargreaves

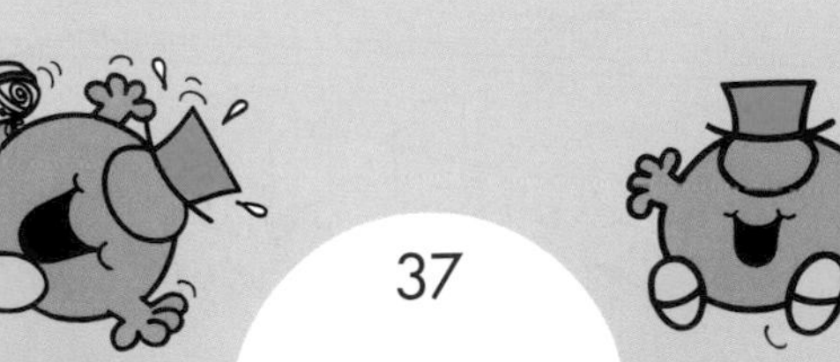

MR. SILLY

Mr Silly lives in Nonsenseland, which is a very funny place to live.

You see, in Nonsenseland, everything is as silly as can be.

In Nonsenseland the trees are red!

And the grass is blue!

Isn't that silly?

In Nonsenseland dogs wear hats!

And do you know how birds fly in Nonsenseland?

No, they don't fly forwards.

They fly backwards!

It really is a very silly place indeed.

Which of course is why Mr Silly lives there.

MR. SILLY

Mr Silly, in fact, lives in quite the silliest looking house you have ever seen in your whole life.

Have you ever seen a sillier looking house than that?

Now, this particular story is all about the Nonsense Cup.

You see, in Nonsenseland each year they hold a competition, and the Cup is awarded to whoever has the silliest idea of the year.

Mr Silly had never won the Cup, but each night, lying in his bed, he dreamed about winning it.

MR. SILLY

In order to win the Nonsense Cup Mr Silly realised that he would have to think up something remarkably silly.

He pondered over the problem one morning at breakfast.

Incidentally, you may be interested to know what Mr Silly was having for breakfast.

He was having a cup of coffee, which he put a spoonful of marmalade into.

After that he had a cornflake sandwich.

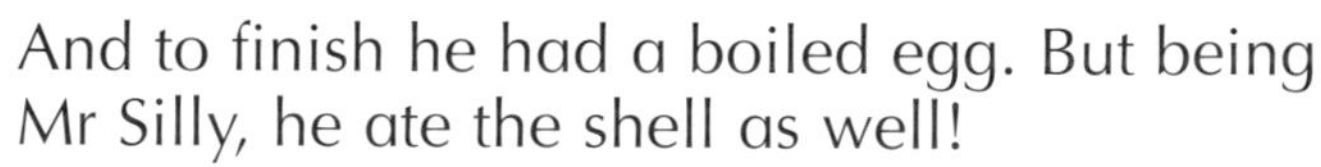

And to finish he had a boiled egg. But being Mr Silly, he ate the shell as well!

Isn't that a silly breakfast!

Anyway this particular breakfast time, Mr Silly was thinking how to win that Cup.

He remembered two years ago the Cup was won by Mr Ridiculous.

He won by wallpapering his house.

Which sounds very ordinary, but in fact Mr Ridiculous had wallpapered the *outside* of his house!

And Mr Silly remembered last year when Mr Foolish won the Cup.

Mr Foolish, who was a friend of Mr Silly's, had won the Cup by inventing a car.

It was quite a normal car, apart from one thing. It had square wheels!

Isn't that silly?

Mr Silly thought and thought and thought, but it was no good.

He even had another cup of coffee with marmalade, but that didn't help either.

So, he decided to take a walk.

Off he went, leaving his front door open so that he wouldn't have burglars when he was out.

On his walk Mr Silly met a chicken wearing wellington boots and carrying an umbrella.

"Wouldn't it be silly if you didn't wear wellington boots and carry an umbrella?" he said to the chicken.

"Meow!" said the chicken, because animals in Nonsenseland don't make the same noises as they do in your country.

On his walk Mr Silly met a worm wearing a top hat, monocle and an old school tie.

"Wouldn't it be silly if you didn't wear a top hat, a monocle and an old school tie?" he said to the worm.

"Quack! Quack!" said the worm.

Next Mr Silly met a pig wearing trousers and a bowler hat.

"Wouldn't it be silly if you didn't wear trousers and a bowler hat?" he asked the pig.

"Moo!" said the pig.

Isn't that silly?

It was in the middle of Mr Silly's walk that he had his idea.

It was a beautifully silly idea.

Quite the silliest idea he'd ever had.

He hurried into town, and bought himself a pot of paint and a paintbrush.

The day of the great awarding of the Nonsense Cup arrived.

A huge crowd assembled in the City Square to see who was going to win the Cup.

The King of Nonsenseland mounted the specially built platform.

"Ladies and gentlemen," he said to the crowd in the City Square. "It is my pleasure today to award the Nonsense Cup to whoever has had the silliest idea of the year."

"One of the silliest ideas of the year," continued the King, "is by Mr Muddle the farmer. He has managed to grow, of all things, a square apple!"

The crowd clapped as the square apple was held up by Mr Muddle for everybody to see.

He felt sure he was going to win.

"However," said the King, and Mr Muddle's face fell, "we have an even sillier idea entered by Mrs Nincompoop."

It was a teapot. Quite the silliest teapot there'd ever been.

The crowd broke into thunderous applause.

"I therefore have great pleasure," announced the King, "in presenting the Nonsense Cup to . . ."

Just then he looked up, and stopped in astonishment.

Now in the middle of the City Square there is a tree.

It's always been there, and it was at this tree that the king was looking in astonishment.

"What," he cried, "has happened to that tree?"

Everybody had turned to look. The tree had green leaves!

Bright green leaves!

Not red leaves like all the trees in Nonsenseland, but green.

There was an amazed silence.

"It was me," piped up Mr Silly. "I painted all the leaves green last night when you were all asleep!"

"A green tree!" exclaimed the King. "Whoever heard of a green tree?"

"A green tree!" shouted the crowd. "How silly!" And they started to applaud.

Mr Silly smiled modestly.

The King held up his hands.

"I think," he said, "that this is the silliest idea I have ever heard of, and therefore I award the Nonsense Cup to Mr Silly!"

The crowd cheered and cheered.

Mr Silly went pink with pride.

And a bird, perched high up in the branches of the silly green tree, looked down.

"Woof!" it said, and flew off, backwards!

MR. SMALL

by Roger Hargreaves

MR. SMALL

Mr Small was very small. Probably the smallest person you've ever seen in your whole life.

Or perhaps the smallest person you've never seen in your whole life, because he was so small you probably wouldn't see him anyway.

Mr Small was about as big as a pin, which isn't very big at all, so perhaps we should say that Mr Small was as small as a pin!

Mr Small lived in a small house underneath a daisy at the bottom of Mr Robinson's garden.

It was a very nice house, although very tiny, and it suited Mr Small very well indeed. He liked living there.

MR. SMALL

Now this story is all about the time Mr Small decided to get a job.

The trouble was, what sort of job could Mr Small do? After all there aren't that many small jobs!

Mr Small had thought about it for a long time, but hadn't had any ideas.

Not one!

He was thinking about it now, while he was having lunch.

He was having half a pea, one crumb, and a drop of lemonade.

Mr Small thought and thought while he was eating his big lunch, but it was no use.

Thinking just made him thirsty, so he had another drop of lemonade.

"I know," he thought to himself. "After lunch I'll go and see Mr Robinson and ask his advice."

So after lunch he left his house and walked to Mr Robinson's house at the top of the garden.

It was quite a long walk for somebody as small as Mr Small, and halfway there he stopped for a rest.

He sat on a pebble feeling quite out of breath.

MR. SMALL

A worm crawled by, and stopped.

"Good afternoon, Mr Small," said the worm.

"Good afternoon, Walter," said Mr Small to the worm, whom he knew quite well.

"Out for a walk are you?" asked Walter.

"Going to see Mr Robinson," replied Mr Small.

"Oh!" said Walter.

"About a job," added Mr Small.

"Oh!" said Walter the worm again, and crawled off.

Walter was a worm of very few words.

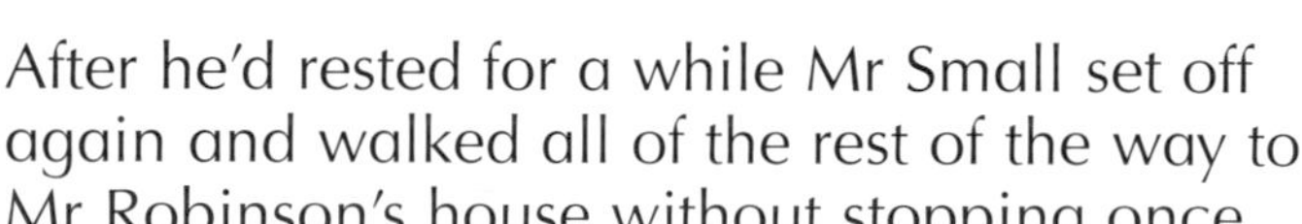

After he'd rested for a while Mr Small set off again and walked all of the rest of the way to Mr Robinson's house without stopping once.

When he got there he climbed up the steps to Mr Robinson's back door.

He knocked at the door.

Nobody heard him!

He knocked again at the door.

Nobody heard him!

The trouble was, you see, that if you're as small as Mr Small you don't have a very loud knock.

MR. SMALL

Mr Small looked up.

There, high above his head, was a doorbell.

"How can I ring the bell when I can't reach it?" thought Mr Small to himself.

He started to climb up the wall, brick by brick, to reach the bell.

He had climbed up four bricks when he made the mistake of looking down.

"Oh dear," he said, and fell.

Bang!!

"Ouch!" said Mr Small, rubbing his head.

Just then Mr Small heard footsteps.

It was the postman.

The postman came to the door, posted his letters, and was just about to leave when he heard a voice.

"Hello," said the voice.

The postman looked down.

"Hello," he said to Mr Small. "Who are you?"

"I'm Mr Small," said Mr Small. "Will you ring the bell for me?"

MR. SMALL

"Of course I will," replied the postman in answer to Mr Small's question, and reaching out he pressed the bell with his finger.

"Thank you," said Mr Small.

"My pleasure," said the postman, and off he went.

Mr Small heard footsteps coming to the door.

The door opened.

Mr Robinson opened the door and looked out.

"That's funny," he said. "I'm sure I heard somebody ring the bell!"

He was about to shut the door when he heard a little voice.

"Hello," said the voice. "Hello, Mr Robinson."

Mr Robinson looked down, and down.

"Hello," he said. "What are you doing here?"

"I've come to ask your advice," said Mr Small to Mr Robinson.

"Well," said Mr Robinson. "You'd better come in and have a talk."

Mr Small followed Mr Robinson into the house, and, perched on the arm of Mr Robinson's favourite chair, he told him how he couldn't think of a job that he could do.

Mr Robinson sipped a cup of tea, and listened.

"So you see," Mr Small explained, "how difficult it is."

"Yes, I can see that," said Mr Robinson. "But leave it to me."

Mr Robinson knew a lot of people.

Mr Robinson knew someone who worked in a restaurant, and arranged for Mr Small to work there.

Putting mustard into mustard pots!

But Mr Small kept falling into the pots and getting covered in mustard, so he left that job.

MR. SMALL

Mr Robinson knew somebody who worked in a sweetshop, and arranged for Mr Small to work there.

Serving sweets!

But Mr Small kept falling into the sweet jars, so he left that job.

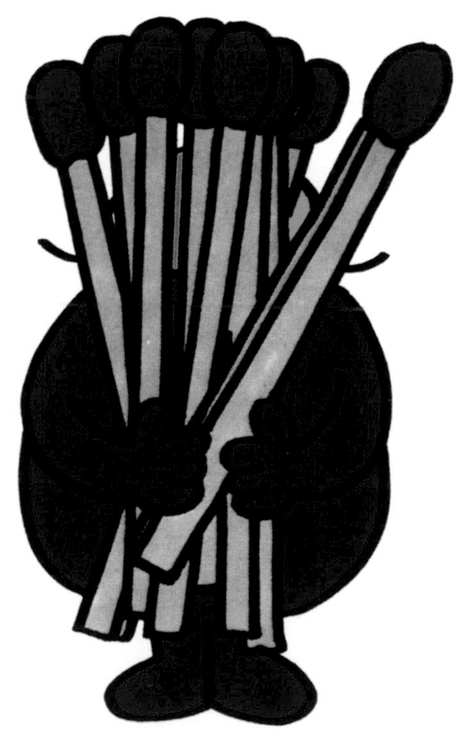

Mr Robinson knew somebody who worked in a place where they made matches, and arranged for Mr Small to work there.

Packing matches into boxes!

But Mr Small kept getting shut in the boxes with the matches, so he left that job.

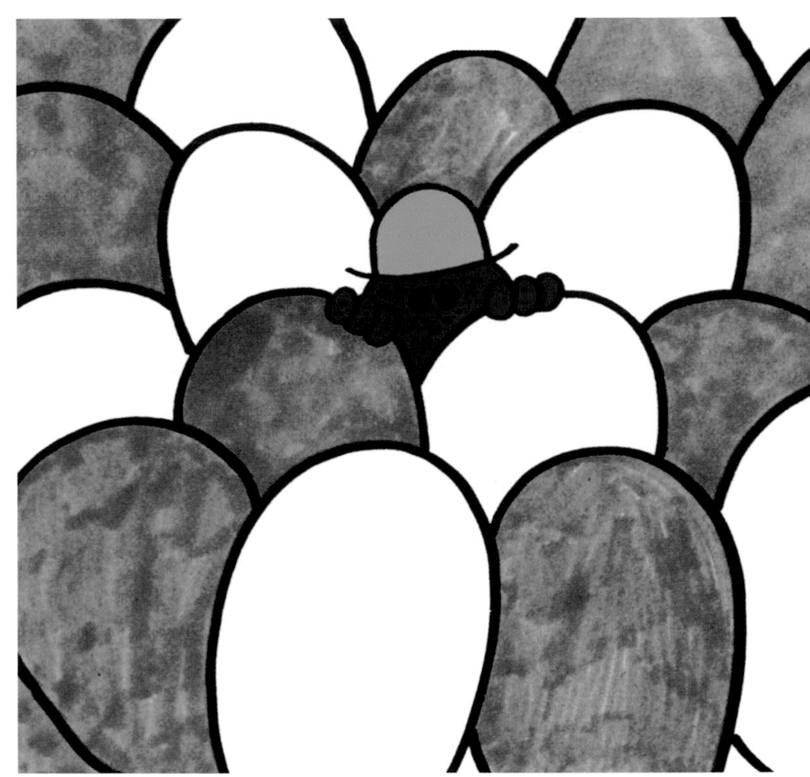

Mr Robinson knew somebody who worked on a farm, and arranged for Mr Small to work there.

Sorting out the brown eggs from the white eggs!

But Mr Small kept getting trapped by the eggs, so he left that job.

"What are we going to do with you?" Mr Robinson asked Mr Small one evening.

"Don't know!" said Mr Small in a small voice.

"I've got one more idea," said Mr Robinson. "I know somebody who writes children's books. Perhaps you could work for him."

MR. SMALL

So the following day Mr Robinson took Mr Small to meet the man who wrote children's books.

"Can I work for you?" Mr Small asked the man.

"Yes you can," replied the man. "Pass me that pencil and tell me all about the jobs you've been doing. Then I'll write a book about it. I'll call it *Mr Small*," he added.

"But children won't want to read all about me!" exclaimed Mr Small.

"Yes they will," replied the man. "They'll like it very much!"

And you did.

Didn't you?

MR. MEN